THE EARL AND THE WITCH

CHLOE WILLOWFIELD

THE EARL AND THE WITCH
First published in Australia in 2026 by Chloe Willowfield

Copyright © 2026 by Chloe Willowfield

All rights reserved.

No part of this publication may be reproduced, distributed, or transmitted in any form or by any means, including photocopying, recording, or other electronic or mechanical methods, without the prior written permission of the publisher. For permission requests, contact Chloe Willowfield via chloe@chloewillowfield.com

This is a work of fiction. Names, characters, places, and incidents either are the product of the author's imagination or are used fictitiously, and any resemblance to actual persons, living or dead, business establishments, events, or locales is entirely coincidental.

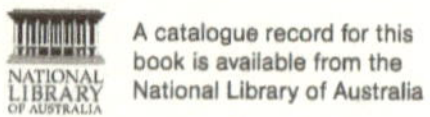

A catalogue record for this book is available from the National Library of Australia

ISBN: 9781763748040
ISBN: 9781763748057 (eBook)

Cover design by Miblart

To MD, the Ding and Sailboat.

CONTENTS

Chapter One

Ava

Here are two facts you should know about me. First, my name is Ava Penrose. And second, I'm a witch.

Not many people know that second tidbit because it's best to keep that sort of information only among fellow magical folk.

I'm going out hiking in a part of the country I've never been to before. Wiltshire. I've heard great things about the stone circles in this part of the country from my fellow witches. Everyone knows, of course, about Stonehenge and Avebury. But there are others, known only to magical folk, with even greater powers. Some of the best places to do magic in all of England.

I really want to find Old Tattersham's Circle today. And conduct several spells that will bring good fortune for the coming year.

This morning, I caught a train from my home in London to the small village of Little Battlington. Request stop only! When I started out for the day, the weather was fine. Clear skies and mild temperatures. The last days of summer were behind us and autumn was settling in. After arriving at Little Battlington, I walked for about an hour across the bridleway that I was sure would lead me to Old Tattersham's Circle. I love seeing the trees begin to turn amber and russet.

But that was earlier. Now, I notice with growing unease that ominous dark clouds are forming in the skies overhead. A storm is brewing.

Cursing, I stop walking and think through my next move. By my calculations I'm closer to Little Battlington than I am to Old Tattersham's Circle. So I am best off turning around and retracing my footsteps back to the station. How frustrating to have to cut my walk short like this! But it would be madness to continue, so turn back I must.

A couple of minutes pass by uneventfully.

Then the heavens start to bucket down. The rain drops are big and heavy, pelting my exposed arms and legs and drenching my hair. As I march on determinedly, the ground begins to get soggier and soggier, becoming pure mud in some places. I struggle to maintain my footing when the icing on the cake of this mistake of a day happens.

Lightning strikes right near me and suddenly all I can see is a flash of white light. Have I died? Then, just as quickly as it appeared, the bright light goes away and I'm thrown to the floor. I glance around hesitantly. It looks like exactly the same place as where I had been a moment before. Only this time there's no sign of any rain. The sky is blue and clear and the ground is dry.

Bemused, I try to get up off the ground but there's a shooting pain in my left hip. I begin to reach for my bag when the beats of horse's hooves fill my ears.

Then there's the almighty sound of a shocked man bellowing at me. "Who on earth are you? No one is supposed to be here! What is the meaning of -"

The horse's hooves and the man's voice both stop.

Then the horse neighs softly.

I hear the man dismount from the horse and walk towards me. Leather riding boots fill my line of vision. Then a wonderful sight meets my eyes. The most gorgeous man I have ever seen. He has a handsome angular face with hawk-like deep brown eyes and dark brown hair. Clean shaven, he wears a navy silk cravat and a black top hat. I gasp internally. He is delicious.

Stop it, I tell myself. You have just had an utterly bizarre experience where one minute you were walking on a mild autumn day, the next you were caught in a storm and now you are laying on the ground on a totally fine day with a very fine sight right in front of you! None of this makes any sense whatsoever!

"Madam," he begins, his voice now even and gentle rather than the frenzied bellowing of earlier, "Can you hear me?"

"Yes," I croak, "Wha-what happened?"

"That's what I'm wondering myself. But before we try to figure that out, I want to make sure you're safe. Are you able to walk?"

"I'm not sure." I try to move but the pain is too great.

"My left hip really hurts."

I go to get up but I flounder. I'm in agony.

"Don't worry, I'll get you on my horse and back to the house." He notices my small rucksack on the floor a little way away from me. It must have fallen off when the lightning strike happened and I ended up on the ground. "Is that yours, madam?"

"Yes," I croak.

"Right." He makes his way towards my bag, reaches down and then returns to place it in my hands.

I look at him more closely, He is dressed very strangely. He looks exactly like something out of a regency film or show. He has the full on regency look going on with the leather riding boots, tight trousers, waistcoat, cravat, long navy blue greatcoat and black top hat. Is he an actor? Is there some sort of production doing filming around these parts? Why else would anyone be riding around dressed like a regency gentleman in this day and age?

In any case, whatever the reason, this regency getup suits him very well indeed. Hopefully I can watch him in whatever movie or show he's filming when it hits the screens.

Then he bends down and picks me up in his arms.

God, I thought, he must be very strong to be able to do that. I'm a grown woman! It feels so good to be in his arms, so strong and safe.

Stop that! I shake my head internally. You are a grown woman. You had an accident in a storm and now your mind is making up this whole weirdly hot scenario as a way to cope. You need to get a grip of yourself and call someone for help!

He carries me to the horse. "Have you ridden before?"

"Not a horse, no," I reply. "I have ridden donkeys a few times though, and a camel once."

He looks down at me and quirks an eyebrow. "A camel? Where did you ride a camel?"

"In Tunisia on holiday as a child. I would've been eight or so, for some reason the tour company took us to an agricultural college and we rode camels there," I say.

Befuddlement crosses his face, followed by a wry smile. "That sounds nice. Well, since you haven't ridden a *horse* before, I'll explain to you what to do. You need to put your bag somewhere first. How does it work?"

This is weird. Why is he asking me how a rucksack worked? But I don't want to be rude. "Oh, I can wear it on my back."

"Right. I'm going to lift you onto the horse, then you'll sit up and I'll get on in front. Once you're on the horse, don't move unless I tell you to."

He lifts me up and asks, "Are you able to put your bag on or would you like some help?"

"I've got it, thank you." I sling my rucksack over my shoulders.

Then he gets on the horse, sitting in front of me.

I like being close to him. It feels comfortable and right.

"I'm sorry madam, this is rather indelicate. But you need to put your hands on my waist so you don't fall off the horse."

I duly do so. He has such a firm line to his body and I enjoy the sensation of him beneath my hands. Stop it! I tell myself sternly. This man is trying to help you and all you are doing now is lusting after him! You need to control yourself!

He grabs the reins. and then we're off at a steady canter. We make our way down the gently sloping hill towards a grand stately home. This must be Varley Hall!

I had been looking forward to seeing it in the distance from my walk, given that the grounds themselves were not public land, but had missed the opportunity due to the storm and the bizarre lightning incident. It cuts an imposing impression on the landscape. As though it owns the earth and had created all that surrounded it. It looks to be a mid-eighteenth century construction from the front, which lined up with the earlier reading I had done on its history.

I had come to learn that Varley Hall was first built in the Elizabethan era for the Earl of Ashendon and was substantially rebuilt during the reign of George II. Today it remains the private residence of the earl and his family and was off limits to the public, save for the bridleway I had been walking along and occasions when the grounds were hired out for filming. Several of my favourite historical films and shows have been made here and I love to watch them again and again to relive the splendour and tradition. What can I say, I am a modern woman in a lot of ways but I am a sucker for that old fashioned luxury and elegance.

We draw up outside a sweeping entrance, replete with two grand staircases.

A man in red livery bursts out of the doors at the top of the lefthand staircase. He runs down the steps in double quick time. "My lord," he shouts.

Is this part of some scene they're filming? Does he think I'm one of the cast?

I look around. This is strange. There are no cameras in sight. These men must be very committed to their craft to stay in character with no camera or crew around.

The man behind me calls back to the liveried man. "Have tea prepared in the yellow drawing room. We have company."

Confusion fills the liveried man's features for a few brief seconds. Then he regains control of himself and his expression neutralises. "At once, my lord."

The man behind me dismounts from the horse. Then he calls up to me, "Here, take my hand."

His palm is firm and sturdy beneath mine. Here and there he has some callouses on his fingers, as though he does something with his hands but doesn't rely on them to make his living.

I dismount the horse, one leg over the other, and land on the ground with a soft thud. The gravel crunches beneath my feet.

Almost immediately, he lets go of my hand. "Please, come inside. My servants will prepare us some refreshments."

I quirk an eyebrow. "And why would I want to do that?"

"Well, you look like you've had a rough time of it, madam. It's the least I could do for someone in a situation such as yours."

I almost splutter a laugh in reply, but the earnestness with which he speaks makes me think better of it. Instead, I follow him down a corridor lined with oil paintings and then into a drawing room.

By now, my hip is beginning to ache less. Mercifully, it seems like it was only a temporary thing.

He gestures at a settee. "Please, have a seat, madam."

I sit down on the settee. It's a formal piece in the Rococo style with pale lemon-satin fabric and white wooden legs and arms.

This is an excellent recreation, I tell myself. Really convincing. If I didn't know any better, I'd think this was a piece from centuries ago. But it's in fine condition, almost new, so surely it has to be a replica. Part of the set for whatever production they're filming here at the moment.

A man in red livery enters the room. He's not the same as the man I saw outside. He's carrying a tea tray. "My lord," he says. Then he places the tea tray on the coffee table, gives a small bow and leaves.

This is weird. Everyone I've seen here on this estate so far is really committed to being part of whatever production it is they're filming. They're method actors to their core.

The man takes a seat opposite me and begins to pour tea. "I hope this will help you to recover your strength, madam. After that tumble you took, a good strong cup of tea will do you wonders." He offers me a cup.

"Oh, um, thank you," I say. I take a sip.

"I'm afraid I haven't yet introduced myself. I'm Ashendon. The tenth Earl of Ashendon," he says.

"Ava Penrose. It's very nice to meet you, Ashendon." My word, this man is committed to his acting bit. It's all I can do but to go along with him.

"Miss Penrose? It is Miss, I presume?"

"Yes, if you like."

"Then I shall call you Miss Penrose. One doesn't feel close enough to be on first name terms yet," he says.

"Oh, yes, as you wish," I say. This man is so prim and proper! Am I having a conversation with some sort of Mr Darcy? I can't say I dislike it. But I definitely did not expect this when I woke up this morning.

He brings his own cup to his lips. Then he asks, "How are you faring, Miss Penrose? You seemed in strife when I found you. You had taken a nasty tumble?"

I shift a little in my seat. I can hardly feel the sting in my hip anymore. "Oh, I'm much better now. Thank you for asking."

He nods gravely. "I'm most glad to hear it. But if you do need any assistance, I can arrange a doctor posthaste."

"Thank you."

He nods again but says nothing.

I drink in the vision of him. He's like something out of a regency film. All fine cut suit with navy coat and white pantaloons and those black hessian boots. A silken cravat adorns his neck, leading up to a very handsome face like Michelangelo might have sculpted back in the day. He's exactly the kind of man who could get a job as an actor.

"So how long are you here for? For this part?" I ask him. Maybe I can get him to drop his method acting and we can have a proper conversation and I can be on my way. If I hurry, I can still get to Old Tattersham's Circle in time for the ritual and the day won't have been wasted after all.

He raises a quizzical eyebrow. "Which part?"

"Oh you know what I mean! The part of the earl you're playing. Ashendon or whatever you said it was."

"Miss Penrose, I can assure you I am no mere man playing a part. I am the Earl of Ashendon." No amusement reaches his eyes. He's either serious or seriously deluded.

I don't know how to reply to that. So I say nothing and instead take another sip of my tea.

The strange yet handsome man keeps his silence too.

We sit, drinking tea and curiously assessing each other, for several minutes. Not a word passes between us.

Until the man who keeps telling me he's an earl finishes his tea and puts his cup down on the table. "Miss Penrose, I have some business to attend to. But when you have had your fill of refreshment, it would be my privilege to assist you. Please excuse me."

He stands up, gives me a bow and hurries out of the room.

This is really weird. What planet is this man on? Planet Austen?

When I finish my tea, I put my cup down and set my mind on getting back on track to Old Tattersham's Circle. I'll quickly review the map to make sure I'm on the right track and then I'll be on my way again. No need to hang around Mr Weirdo Darcy.

I take out my phone from the innermost pocket of my rucksack.

I turn it on and unlock it. My familiar screensaver with two tabby cats and a spellbook greets me. It's good to see something familiar when I'm in such a bizarre situation.

But not one bar of signal!

One thing I had not banked on was the lack of mobile phone reception out here. Not being from the countryside, I had wrongly assumed things like phone reception worked the same way here as they did in towns. But I was wrong.

That's what I get for coming to the countryside unprepared, I suppose. That and an encounter with a strangely handsome man who can only be an actor or some sort of roleplayer who is determinedly committed to his craft.

I put my phone back in my bag. Surely a place like this has a landline. They can't be that disconnected from civilization!

I cast my eyes around the room. It's beautifully ornate but no sign of any landline. There's no point in staying here. I need to call someone and sort out how to get back to Little Battlington. I can probably get a taxi to take me to the station, though that is going to take a while.

Figuring the hallway is as good a place as any to start my search, I make my way through the heavy oaken door and out onto gleaming black and white tiles.

There isn't immediately a phone in sight. But no matter. I'm sure I'll find one.

I keep walking, past rows and rows of stuffy portraits. I'm no great art historian but from what I can tell based on how the people are dressed, those portraits are from the Stuart and Georgian eras. Nothing more recent than that. Well, that would make sense if this house is being used as a film set. Production would've taken down any pictures more recent than the Regency. Otherwise, there would've been far too modern pictures lurking in the background of a scene that was meant to take place in 1816. That would have made for a silly sight!

I'm nearing the end of the hallway now and still no telephone in view.

Before I reach the end, a man's voice calls out to me. "Ah, there you are!"

The weirdly handsome man from earlier appears from a nearby doorway.

I nod at him.

"I trust everything is to your satisfaction?" he asks.

"It is, yes," I reply. "Though I need to head back to Framlington. Could I use your phone please? I'll call for a cab."

His brow scrunches in a brief moment of confusion. "Oh there's no need to trouble yourself. I can have one of my men take you down in the carriage. You can leave within the half hour."

The carriage? That's a strange way of putting it! This man is really committed to his method acting.

I nod. "That would be good, thank you."

"Consider it done." The man turns on his heel and heads off to what I can only presume is to arrange a car to take me to Framlington.

With not much better to do, I head back to the drawing room. I make my way over to a tall oaken bookcase and cast my eyes over rows and rows of thick tomes. Maybe I can find something to peruse while I wait for the car.

But before I get a chance to pick some reading material, a bright flash of pain sears through my head.

What's happening? I don't normally get migraines.

Is this the result of a spell going wrong?

I chant a healing incantation over and over.

Another flash of pain.

I keep chanting the healing incantation but it's not working.

I take several deep breaths. Though all to no avail.

I groan in agony. My head is growing fuzzy and I'm feeling weaker and weaker. Sleep seems like a fantastic idea right now.

I can't think of much else.

The world turns black.

Chapter Two

Ava

I open my eyes. Bright white light floods the room.

What happened? Did I pass out from what was the worst headache I'd ever had in my life?

I look around me. But instead of the bookshelves I'm expecting to see, the four posters of a voluminous bed greet my eyes.

This is totally bizarre. What happened? Why am I in this bed?

Groggily, I raise myself up onto my elbows and lean forwards for a better look at my surroundings.

A woman in a maroon dress is sitting in a chair on the other side of the room. She sees me sit up and her lips form a small smile. "At last, Mistress! You are awake! It's been several days. You gave us all quite a scare. You are awake! Oh, this is wonderful news. I will let his lordship know."

His lordship?

Before I can form a reply, the woman darts up from her chair and disappears through a door to who knows where.

Who on earth was she? And why didn't she talk to me like a normal person? Why all the ye olden days talk?

Today is getting stranger and stranger. And I'm a witch, so nothing should surprise me.

For want of anything better to do, I get out of the bed. My feet pad on luxurious rugs. This certainly *feels* like a Regency country house.

Whoever designed the sets did a fantastic job.

But this is surely only a set. For some show or film.

A glinting mirror across the room catches my eye. I head over to it and meet my own gaze. My face looks about the same as ever but I'm wearing a strange, billowing white nightdress. The kind of thing someone last wore back in my grandmother's youth. I hold the cotton of the dress between my fingers. Yuck! It wouldn't be my choice of clothing, that's for sure. Whyever did someone put me in this? So weird!

In my reflection I spot a wardrobe behind me. Perhaps there's something better in there.

I make my way to the heavy oaken cabinet and open the doors. Several dresses greet my eyes. Ah ha! Here's the dress I wore when I arrived. My favourite purple number. And my faithful boots too!

I reach forward in excitement and put them on. Then I turn back to the mirror. That's better. I look more like myself again.

That business over, it's time to find someone and figure out exactly what on earth is going on and how I can get back home. I don't want to hang around in a place like this a minute longer than I need to.

I stride out the room. I'm a woman on a mission.

A few minutes later and I've found him. The man who brought me to this house. The one who seems to think he's playing Mr Darcy.

He looks good. But will he help me? Or is he going to keep up his bizarre pretence from before.

His eyes widen when he sees me. "Miss Penrose! There you are. Oh yes, Lottie mentioned you had awoken. How are you faring?"

So he still wants to keep up his stupid act. Well, I need to get home. I don't have time for his fun and games. Best I cut to the chase. "I need to get to Framlington. I've been away from home for far too long and people will be missing me," I say.

"I wish I could get you a carriage posthaste. But, regrettably, there are heavy floods coming in. The roads out will all be blocked for weeks," he says with genuine concern in his voice.

"What?" I say in disbelief.

"We've had an unusually wet summer. I haven't seen the like since before I became the earl."

I'm distracted from the talk of the weather by this latest attempt at acting. How long is he going to keep this up, for heaven's sake! "The earl?"

"Yes" he replies in a tone like everyone should know this information already. "I am the tenth Earl of Ashendon."

I scrunch up my nose a little. I suppose he did already tell me that. But it's gotten to the point of ridiculousness. This guy's method acting is wearing really thin right now. "You mean you're an actor playing the tenth Earl of Ashendon." His eyebrows shoot up. "No, madam. I can assure you I am no mere actor. I am the Earl of Ashendon."

"And I'm Queen of the May!"

"Well, then, Queen of the May, I am very pleased to meet you," he retorts, his voice as smooth as silk.

I don't respond for several beats. Either this guy is a liar or he is insane or he really is the earl.

I cross my arms. "Okay, if you're the earl, then prove it."

"Very well. Follow me." He turns on his heel and strides out of the room, not looking back.

I splutter internally. The arrogance of that man. Expecting me to follow. But follow I do.

He leads me out into a hallway, down a flight of stairs and into a grand hall. All around, lining every wall, are rows and rows of portraits. The oldest are in medieval gear.

He gestures as he leads me along. "The first earl, lasted from 1400 to 1440. The second. And the third, he was at the Battle of Bosworth."

On and on he leads me past portraits of men, all severe and aristocratic. Until eventually he gestures to one, dressed in late eighteenth century garb. "My uncle, the ninth earl." The man in that portrait bears an awfully similar resemblance to the guy standing in front of me. They do look related, I'll give him that.

He takes a few more steps and then we're in front of a face I unfortunately know all too well by now. "Which brings me to myself. Earl since 1806."

I gaze up at the portrait. There's no denying who it is. But 1806, did he say? That's ridiculous. I can't have travelled back in time. Doing that would require magic far beyond my current capabilities. And I would surely have felt the presence of any other magical beings in the vicinity.

I look back at the man who calls himself 'the tenth earl of Ashendon'. I give him my hardest stare. "Well, I shall have to take you at your word."

He gives a barely perceptible nod. "You shall have to, Queen of the May. But, pray tell, who are you really?"

"Who am I?"

"Yes. Who are you? You seem awfully reluctant to believe me when I tell you I'm the earl. And, I'm sorry to say, I don't believe you are the Queen of the May. That's a ludicrous title."

Arrogant and rude! This man! "Whoever I am, it's no business of yours. I need to leave immediately," I say, drawing myself up to my full height.

"Madam, the rains are on their way. The roads will be flooded out for weeks. It is the least I can do to host you here."

I sigh internally. Something about this guy tells me he isn't lying. Which makes this situation hard to navigate. I'll do my best to make him think like I'm taking him at his word. But I'll try to find a way back to my time with my magic.

He looks expectantly at me for a response.

"Well, I thank you for your kind hospitality," I say.

"You're most welcome. And you haven't answered my question. Who are you really?"

"Miss Ava Penrose," I offer.

"It's very nice to meet you, Miss Ava Penrose." He gives a formal bow.

"Thank you," I say guardedly. I can't let him know I'm a witch. I have no idea how he might take it. We aren't always well liked even today, let alone whatever era this man thinks he's in. The early 1800s! It seems so ridiculous.

"I'll have the servants set up some proper rooms for you. The East Wing should suit you well."

"Oh, thank you."

We both stand in silence for a few seconds.

Part of me doesn't really believe it's the early 1800s. I need proper proof.

An idea bursts into my head. It wouldn't hurt to ask him, surely? Even if indirectly? Would it? Throwing caution to the wind, I say, "Do you get much news from outside here? Would it be possible to read the latest? After my illness, I fear I am behind the times."

He nods. "Yes, I've got some pamphlets and newspapers in my study. If you'd like to follow me." He gestures down the corridor.

Once we're in his office, he points at a heavy mahogany desk. It's teeming with paperwork and books.

"Take your pick, Miss Penrose," he says.

I pick up the first one from his desk. *The Times*. Dated the First of July, 1816. And then another. The Second of July, 1816. And another. Each looks fresh, like it was only printed a week ago and hasn't seen the ravages of time.

I cast my eyes over the rest of his desk. Some sort of letter from Lord Melbourne. And another from Earl Grey.

Nothing in this room looks aged but it's all from the early nineteenth century.

As much as I want to deny it, that strange yet weirdly handsome man seems to be telling the truth.

He really is an earl. And it really is 1816.

That's all well and good for him. But not to me.

If I do nothing else, I need to find a way back to my own time. I'm a modern witch. Not some regency debutante, after all.

But he can't know what I'm up to. If this is to succeed, I'm going to have to be discreet.

I turn to where he is standing.

He's watching me intently. He's as wary of me as I am of him. "I trust you have found what you need, Miss Penrose?" he asks.

"Oh, yes, thank you." I don't want to give too much away. I'll have to go along with the ruse.

He nods and a small smile forms on his features. "I'm very glad to hear it."

<hr>

Back in the guest room, I haven't the first idea where to start with how to get back home. This whole situation is a mess.

I sigh to myself. I'm getting caught in useless spirals.

I take five deep breaths to centre my mind. What I need to do is think clearly.

I sit like that in silence, focusing my mind on calmness and not needing to rush. I don't know how many minutes have passed when something useful pops into my head. I know a place to start. Something that's going to be helpful.

What I need to do is think through all the magic I've ever learned. The lessons at Spellpath Academy. Every spellbook I've read over the years. Once I put everything together, I'll be in a better position to find my way back to the twenty-first century.

This is going to take some time and some planning.

I reach inside my rucksack and retrieve my notepad. It's time to get cracking.

I've got pages and pages of notes in front of me.

The lessons I remember from the Academy with Grand Witch Reynolds. She said there were legends of time travelling centuries ago. Back in Ancient Greece. But they are only legends and no witch alive has successfully time travelled, though a not insignificant number have tried.

If I spend enough time on this, surely I can push through and find a solution. Find a way home. Find a way back to my own time.

I cannot give up hope. But I know that today isn't going to be my day.

So until I find a spell to send me home, the least I can do at a time like this is to try and get the rains to clear up. If I get them to stop, then the road may open and I can try getting to one of the villages near here and then somehow find my way to one of the great witching cities like York. And there, perhaps, by some shred of chance, I may find more information that can help me find my way back home and meet with one of the witches there, one of the learned ones, with decades of experience who could tell me more. And even if they haven't been able to travel through time themselves, they could point me in the right direction.

So I rack my brain for some of the enchantment charms I know to bring on good weather. Yes, I've got one that comes to mind. I grab a cloak and wrap it around my shoulders. This sort of enchantment needs to take place outside. And the best place is under an arbor of trees, so that's where I'm going to head.

CHAPTER THREE

AVA

Rain patters down the lead lined windows of what is now my new bedroom. The earl gave it to me, telling me it's the best guest suite in the house and to please forgive him for the lack of renovations. I don't care about that. It all looks incredibly luxurious to me.

We've had a couple of days of this nonstop rain. There's nothing else to do other than stay inside. My phone still doesn't work and I can only believe that it's really 1816.

I've racked my brains for anything I can remember about how to get home, back to my own time. But I've come up with nothing so far. I've only been a witch for a couple of years and there's so much I still don't know. Maybe if I was an experienced witch of several decade's standing, I would have already figured out a way back and left this place and time by now. But I am Ava Penrose, the most junior member of the Flambe Circle, and I am out of my depth and out of my time.

The best I can aim for is to get the rains to stop and then maybe I can get to one of the great witching centres, like York or Canterbury and then hopefully find someone who can help me there.

Right now, the rain isn't ceasing and all I can do is try what charms I can to make it stop.

I am lost in my thoughts when there's a cough behind me.

I turn and see where the noise came from. The earl meets my eyes.

"Excuse me, Miss Penrose. I trust everything is to your satisfaction?" he asks.

I nod. "Oh yes, yes, thank you."

"I am glad to hear it." He waits a beat. "Say, would you care to join me for a game of cards? In the drawing room?"

I suppose there's not much else to do on a rainy day such as this. So I give him a nod of agreement. He's probably at just as much of a loose end as I am. Hopefully a game of cards will kill some time if nothing else.

***

A few minutes later and we're sitting facing one another at a small card table in the drawing room.

We're about to play Beat Your Neighbours Out of Doors. I do know how to play, but haven't done so since before I went to the magical academy. I think some people call it Beggar My Neighbour. But we always called it Beat Your Neighbours Out of Doors in my family.

Ashendon reaches for the deck of cards. "Ready?" he asks.

"Of course I am," I reply with a smirk. "The more important question is, are you?"

He gives a curt nod. "Ready as I'll ever be, Miss Penrose." He starts shuffling.

His well formed hands make precise, controlled movements. This is a man who knows how to handle himself.

Once the pack is well and truly shuffled to within an inch of its life, Ashendon grins and starts dealing the cards out in quick, practiced movements.

One for him. One for me. One for him. One for me.

In little more than the blink of an eye, the deck is gone and we each have a pile of cards before us.

The air feels almost ceremonious as we square our decks.

The clock on the mantlepiece ticks softly.

"After you, Miss Penrose," Ashendon says. He's trying to be the perfect gentleman.

I reach over and flip my top card onto the centre of the table. "Six," I call.

Ashendon turns his first card over. "Seven."

We take turns, building a rhythm.

I put down an eight.

Then he puts down a four.

A nine for me.

And on and on and on.

Each card lands with a soft snap that fills the quiet room.

Then luck strikes. For me. I lay down a Queen. "Face card. Pay up. Four chances," I say.

Ashendon grimaces good-naturedly and begins flipping his penalty cards. "One...two..." He pauses dramatically before the third card. "Three! Oh, a Knave!"

"Typical," I mutter.

Now Ashendon takes control. "It seems you owe me one, Miss Penrose."

I start turning cards again. "Two of hearts."

"Seven of clubs."

"King! Lady Fortune has smiled in my favour again!" I shout in glee and slap the card down on the table.

The pile of cards before us is growing messy. It's a jumble of royalty and numbers in red and black.

Ashendon leans forward, his eyes filled with intent, as he sees the situation tilt out of his favour again. He flips a few more cards over. Two. Nine. Five. But no face card.

"That's four," I say in triumph. I sweep the pile towards me and stack it beneath my own deck.

"You are most infuriating, Miss Penrose," Ashendon mutters.

"It's mere talent," I reply in my sweetest voice.

We start throwing cards down again. This time, the battle drags on longer. Sequences of numbered cards pile up on the growing heap in the middle of the table.

We're in a drought of royalty. We haven't had any face cards for almost a full minute.

Then Ashendon draws a King. He slaps it down with theatrical relish. "Pay four!"

I groan and start turning my own cards. Three. Six. Oh and here's something very welcome! A Queen. "Yes! Yes! Yes! The Queen breaks it!"

Ashendon sits back and mock sighs as I take over.

The pile of cards is now thick enough that when I flip the next few cards, the sound of each one landing is sharp, echoing slightly in the otherwise almost silent drawing room.

Eventually, I turn another Queen.

Ashendon can't answer with any face card.

The pile is mine again. I drag the heap towards me. "Told you. It's the luck of Lady Fortune. My kind of luck."

Ashendon stretches his arms. "This game's rigged."

"Ah, Lady Fortune, she smiles down on me."

The next round begins. Cards snap. Laughter rises. It doesn't really matter who's winning or losing. Instead, the room is alive with the simple rhythm of cards, luck and friendly rivalry.

After we've been playing Beat Your Neighbours Out of Doors for an hour with plenty of wins and losses on each side, the temperature in the room starts to drop.

The earl turns his head towards the imposing fireplace a few feet away. The flames are dying down and soon enough there will be mere sparks left in the grate. Only a sullen orange glow spills across the hearthrug.

I begin to raise myself from my chair.

"Do not worry, Miss Penrose, I will get it," he says. With that, he strides across to the fireplace. He kneels down and puts a few more logs on.

He pushes them around with a poker, coaxing them back to life.

The poker rings softly against the fire grate, a measured rhythm.

I can't help myself but make my way over towards him. It's like there's some sort of magnetic pull tonight. Something supernatural.

I crouch beside him and reach for the poker. "Allow me."

His lips quirk up in the smallest hint of a smile. "If you insist, Miss Penrose."

I take the poker and his hands brush against mine. There's a brief, unmistakable frisson of a spark. It's warm. Startling.

Neither of us move for several seconds. The world seems to hold its breath. It's as though just the two of us here, in this room and nothing else matters.

Then, the crackle of the flames suddenly roars in the stillness between us.

The moment breaks. I don't know what to say. It's too awkward to stay around here any longer. With this man who is from two hundred years before my time. However much of a frisson of a spark I felt, it doesn't change the fact that I don't belong here. Nothing can happen between us. Nothing will ever happen between us. I will make sure of it.

Without a word, I raise myself from the floor and move towards the door. I pause for a few seconds to glance back at the earl.

He's still kneeling in front of the fireplace. He looks at me with an unspoken question in his eyes. But not a word passes his lips.

Before I change my mind, I walk out of the room and leave him alone with the restless, newly kindled flames.

CHAPTER FOUR

AVA

Every day the same. Every day it rains.

It's been a week since the earl showed me his evidence that it's 1816. And in that time, I've seen nothing to contradict this fact.

There's not much else we can do when a torrent is blasting the house from all sides.

We're in the drawing room again today.

I make my way towards the piano. It's one of those grand ones. White, with blue and cream swirls around the legs. It's got that rococo look. Ashendon follows behind me.

"Do you play?" he asks.

"A little," I say. "I had lessons for about seven years when I was younger. But I was never the most skilled at it."

"Ah, why not?" he asks, a slight quirk in his eyebrow.

"Well, let's just say I wasn't the most diligent student of music," I reply.

"Nor was I," he says.

"Ah, so you play too?" I ask.

"Yes, like you, a little. My mother, she focused more on giving my sisters lessons, making sure they had a piano tutor, but I used to get to join in too sometimes."

An idea forms in my head. "Would you play for me?"

"As long as you're prepared for it," he says, with a self-depreciating smirk.

He pulls out the piano stool. It's like the piano, it's white, with blue and cream swirls. It's a rather gaudy piece that stands out in the rest of this more classical drawing room.

His fingers find the ivories, and he begins to play a piece, but I'm not sure what it is. It's melodic, and quite lively, unlike the dreary day outside, where the rain continues to pitter-patter down the windows.

"What's that you're playing?" I ask.

He gives a name.

It's not someone I've heard of. Seven years of piano lessons, and I know all the main names like Mozart, Beethoven and Debussy. Well, Debussy, he wasn't even born yet. But you know what I mean. Whoever he's playing probably quite an obscure composer. And magic's long been more my bag than music.

"Nice playing," I say.

He nods in thanks.

I stand and listen to him for a few more minutes, and then he wraps up the piece.

"Say, Miss Penrose, would you like to take a turn?" he asks.

"Alright, as long as you're ready," I say.

"It will be my privilege," he replies.

We swap, so now I'm on the seat, and he's standing by the piano. I don't know if what I'm about to do is going to ruin some timeline, if I'm going to create some sort of butterfly effect, where if I play a more modern song to a man who's still living in the Regency era, it's going to tear a rip in the space-time continuum and I'm never going to be able to get back because I've changed the future irrevocably. But what the heck. I start playing a film score. You'd know it if you heard it.

Ashendon raises his eyebrows slightly.

I can tell he's not familiar with it. Well, why would he be? He was born a hundred years before anyone who ever made this sort of music ever even conceived of it.

"That's, um, different," he says.

"Oh, you don't like it?" I say.

"No, no. In fact, it's rather refreshing. Is it one of your own compositions, Miss Penrose?" he asks.

"I wish it was," I laugh. "Would you like to come and join me? We could play together?"

"I would like that very much indeed."

We sit together side by side on the stool.

My skirts brush against his legs. This is like something out of one of those Regency romance novels. I wonder if he notices.

My fingers move up and down the keys. I'm not really playing anything in particular, just tinkling around.

"That's a sweet melody," he says.

Then he leans forward and plays himself. His piece intersects with mine. They're not quite the same. Mine is more lively and spry, and his is more serious. But together they work. I'm not really sure what you call this type of music, but I like it.

He speeds up his pace a little bit. His rhythm starts to match mine. But he's on the deep notes and my playing is on the much higher part of the piano. Now instead of our intersecting contrast, our playing and our pieces match.

"We go together quite well, don't we Miss Penrose?" he says with a wry note in his voice.

"Yes, I believe we do, Ashendon." A little laugh escapes from me.

"Oh, pray tell, what do you find so amusing?" he asks.

"Well, I'm merely thinking about how well we go together even though we've only known each other a few weeks. And how playing this piano can bring us together. You being an earl and I being Miss Penrose," I say.

"Yes, you're exactly right," he says.

With that, we keep playing the piano together. The tune swells and fills the room with the sound of two people, once strangers but now something more, playing together in harmony.

The next day, I walk into the drawing room.

He's standing at the windows, his back turned to me. But he must have heard me enter because he turns around.

Exasperation clouds his voice. "I'm sick of this."

"Sick of what, Ashendon?" I ask.

"This rain. I can't stand it," he replies. "It's just stopping everything. I have so many responsibilities. I'm supposed to go out and see the tenants. I need to talk to the curate. I know you still wanted to get back to Little Battlington. And none of this, none of this I can do, none of this I can provide for anyone. How am I supposed to do my earldom duties when I'm just reined in here?"

I walk towards him. "I don't think there's anything you can really do to change any of it, unfortunately. I think everyone knows you're doing what you can. But we're all in the same boat here. No one can go anywhere because of the rain."

He sighs. "Miss Penrose, I know you have a point and I know you mean well. But I'm born to be the Earl. And when I can't do my duties, when I can't look after my tenants, when I can't manage my estates properly, when I can't meet with the curate, when I can't even organise a carriage for you to safely get to Little Battlington, I just feel like I'm failing in everything. Failing at being the Earl."

I want to reach out and touch him to provide some comfort, and I'm not sure why. We're just here together in his house until the rain clears and I can somehow get back home, back to my own time. So I force myself not to reach out. Instead, I say, "I don't think there's anything you can do. And I'd stop this rain if I could, but please don't worry about me, Ashendon. You've got enough on your plate already."

He looks down at me through his dark hooded eyes. "Miss Penrose, I will always worry about you."

CHAPTER FIVE

AVA

I make my way down the hallway to the library and sigh to myself. I've been trying these enchantment spells to bring on good weather for days now and it doesn't seem to be having much effect. Here and there, there is a break in the clouds, so my magic is not completely without result. But I think there would need to be a hundred of me to bring about a proper stop to all this rain we keep having.

Whatever's causing this, whatever natural phenomenon, it's far more powerful than my magic is. Yet maybe, maybe if I keep at it I can chip away at whatever's causing this rain and eventually make it stop. It's worth a try.

Perhaps there's something in the library that will help me find my way back home.

I arrive outside its doors and creep inside.

Ashendon is already there, sitting in a winged armchair.

He looks up from the book he's reading. "Miss Penrose, to what do I owe the pleasure?" He lifts himself to his feet and sketches me a bow.

Well there go my plans of rootling around for any magical tomes here today. I'll need to come up with a good excuse.

"Oh, I thought I might see what books you've got here. Any good reading material?"

His eyes brighten at my line of questioning. "This is one of the finest libraries in the county, if I do say so myself. What are you interested in?"

"Well what would you recommend?"

The brightness in his eyes grows. "I'm glad you asked." He heads to an imposing bookshelf and grabs a hefty leather tome. He quickly examines the cover. "Ah yes, this is the one," he says.

"Oh, what is it?" I ask.

"One of Shakespeare's classics," he says.

"Oh right, well I've studied some Shakespeare before."

He carries the book towards me and then sits down in the chair opposite me with it.

"Well, here's one of my favourites of his and I'd like to read it for you," he says.

"Go on then," I reply.

"Double, double toil and trouble, fire burn and cauldron bubble,

Fillet of a fenny snake, in the cauldron boil and bake."

His deep tones reverberate around the room. He's reading it very well and ordinarily I'd enjoy this. He is a very good public speaker, I can tell.

But of all the blasted plays by Shakespeare, why on earth did he pick this one? Macbeth. It's so on the nose. He could have read Romeo and Juliet or A Midsummer Night's Dream or even one of the histories. But no, he has to pick the very one that has the most content about witches in it. And not only are there witches in it, there are also malicious vile old hags in those immortal lines, double double toil and trouble. That's something I've tried to get away from my whole time as a witch ever since I started at Spellpath Academy. Most of the time I've succeeded. But now, through no fault of his own, he's brought forth one of the worst witch stereotypes possible.

As he finishes reading the passage, his eyes lift from the page and he looks at me expectantly.

I can tell he's waiting for some sort of review of his reading. And given that this was completely unintentional on his part, I don't have the heart to raise any issues with the text.

"Oh, I loved that," I reply. Because it's true, I would have really loved it had he read some other Shakespeare play. One of the things like Romeo, Romeo, wherefore art thou? Or a stanza from A Midsummer Night's Dream. But he picked one of the worst ones for someone like me.

"Would you read some more," I say. "What about Lady Macbeth's monologue? Out damn'd spot?"

"Oh yes." He flicks to a different part of the hefty tome and finds it. Then he begins to read.

This part isn't about witches, so it's less on the nose for me. But, to my surprise, the fact that it's from a play about witches still strikes a negative not. I can't get past the horrible image of those stereotypical villainous hags. So unlike the witches I know or the witch I try to be myself.

In any case, it's not his fault that he chose to read such an unfortunate passage for someone like me. I think it's better if he reads from a different play, because I do like how he's performing this piece, just not the content. When he wraps up that passage, I say, "Bravo, bravo!"

He gives me a smile of acknowledgement.

I lean forward in my chair. "Is Macbeth your favourite of Shakespeare's plays?" I ask.

"No. I'm much more partial to A Midsummer Night's Dream."

"How about you read some of that to me then?" I say.

He gives me a curt nod. "Your wish is my command."

He walks over to the bookcase and replaces Macbeth with A Midsummer Night's Dream in his hands. Then he opens the book and begins to read aloud.

"I know a bank where the wild thyme blows,
Where oxlips and the nodding violet grows,
Quite over-canopied with luscious woodbine,
With sweet musk-roses and with eglantine:
There sleeps Titania sometime of the night,
Lulled in these flowers with dances and delight."

He finishes reading the last passage from A Midsummer Night's Dream. Then he closes the book. "You've heard so much of me reading Miss Penrose. How about you read something aloud?"

I say, "Sure, it would be my pleasure." I head over towards the bookcase where he's got a vast collection of works.

I scan through the titles. So many choices. Until my eyes fall on a very familiar classic. Sense and Sensibility.

A perfect choice. I take the book in my hands and head back towards Ashendon.

"I hope you like this one," I say.

I open the book and thumb through. Oh yes, here it is, one of my favourite passages. I begin to read.

"Elinor could sit it no longer. She almost ran out of the room, and as soon as the door was closed, burst into tears of joy, which at first she thought would never cease..."

His eyes remain on me, his gaze intent and focused. Once I finish reading the passage, he says, "You seem to know this one quite well. Are you a fan of that author?"

"Yes, some of her works." But I don't want to reveal much more to him, because I can't exactly remember when each of them were published and I have a suspicious feeling that some of them came out after 1816, so I really don't want to arouse any suspicions from him that I'm a woman out of my time. So, instead, I ask him another question.

"Do you read her?" I ask.

"Only a bit of Pride and Prejudice," he replies. "And to be honest, I'm not really one for novels. That's more for the estate stewards."

"Ah, I see."

"And really," he continues, "Ever since The Sorrows of Young Werther by Goethe, I haven't really had the taste for novels. Goethe put me off."

I let forth a small laugh. "Yes, I had to read that too once. It was such heavy going and so depressing."

"I quite agree with you, Miss Penrose," he says. "But, that passage you've just read to me from, what was it?" "

"Sense and Sensibility," I provide.

"Yes, Sense and Sensibility," he continues. "I found that most emotive. Maybe I'll give it another try at some point."

I've closed Sense and Sensibility and put it back on the shelf, and I scan my eyes over some of his other tomes. "You've got quite a bit of poetry here, Ashendon."

"Oh yes, now poetry, that's... After Shakespeare, that's my main literary love," he says.

"Ah, well, I can read some to you if you like," I reply.

"Yes, yes, please do," he says.

I find a familiar name. The collected works of Ben Johnson. Now Johnson I know because we had to study some of his stuff at school back when I was a teenager.

"Do you like Ben Johnson?" I ask.

"Yes, I like a lot of the poems from those Elizabethan times," he says.

"Oh, how about this one?" I say. Then I begin to read aloud To Celia by Johnson.

"Drink to me only with thine eyes,
*   And I will pledge with mine;*
Or leave a kiss but in the cup,
*   And I'll not look for wine..."*

CHAPTER SIX

ASHENDON

Yet another night of atrocious weather.

Neither Miss Penrose nor myself can find any rest due to the abominable storm that's enwrapping the house in a howling inferno. So it comes as no surprise that we've holed ourselves up in the library in an effort to distract ourselves from our mutual insomnia.

A pot of tea steams on the table before us.

I reach for a cup and fill it with the hot brew. Then I pass the cup over to Miss Penrose before pouring my own.

"I don't know about you," I begin, "but I find that a pot of tea can help when I can't sleep."

"It's worth a shot, Ashendon," she says. She takes a sip of her tea. "It's so hard to relax sometimes, though."

I nod. "I know what you mean. There is always something to keep one's mind a-racing when it's the middle of the night and one wants nothing more than to somehow find some rest."

"You speak like a man with a lot of experience in the subject."

"I do. A great deal, I am sorry to say."

She nods. "And do you ever find any rest?"

"Sometimes. But..." I trail off. I don't relish the thought of admitting to her that even when I do get to sleep, the dreams I often have make me wish I were still awake.

"But?"

I sigh. "But I usually dream. And they're not dreams one wishes to remember. But I do not want to burden you with my problems, Miss Penrose. You're the poor soul stuck here, after all."

"I promise you, you're not burdening me," she says.

"I'm glad to hear it." I cough circumspectively. This isn't right. I'm the host and I'm the earl. It's not right for me to unload my problems onto her. Instead, if she has any difficulties or troubles then she can share them with me and I as the earl will endeavour to fix them. That's my role. That's what I was born to do.

Before I get the chance to formulate another sentence, she fires a question at me.

"So, what do you dream of?"

"Pardon, Miss Penrose?"

"What do you dream of? What are these dreams you don't wish to remember?"

"Running the estate and everything going wrong. Letting down everyone who depends on me, all the tenants and my family. When I became the earl five years ago, after my uncle died, I was fairly well prepared. As much as a man of eight and twenty can be. But I still fear not knowing what I'm doing and making some catastrophic error," I say.

"Ashendon, I've only known you for a little while, but from all I've seen of you, I can't imagine you'd be able to make such a catastrophic error," she says. "You're one of the most diligent and proper men I've ever met."

"I suppose I should take that as a compliment."

She laughs a little. "Well, I did mean it as one."

"Then thank you, Miss Penrose. I mean it."

She smiles before taking another sip of her tea. "You mentioned your uncle? So your father wasn't the earl before you?"

I shake my head. "No, my father was never the earl. He was the younger brother of my uncle but he died many years ago and I was largely raised by my mother and my grandmother. My uncle died childless, leaving me as the heir, you see."

"That must've been a shock. To become earl so unexpectedly," she says sympathetically.

"It was."

"Like I said, though, you are one of the most diligent men I've ever met. So I can't imagine you ever letting your tenants down." She waits a beat and takes a sip of her tea. "You've never let me down."

I blink. Did she really just say that? She thinks I've never let her down? But I most certainly have let her down. I haven't been able to find a way to get her to Little Battlington and now she's stuck on my estate for however long we're flooded out. "Miss Penrose, you are most kind. But I fear I have failed you. I can't even get you over to Little Battlington."

"Ashendon, you are hardly to blame for the weather," she says.

"I know," I sigh. "I still can't help blaming myself though, however irrational it is." I take a sip of my tea. "Anyway, enough about me. What keeps you up at night, Miss Penrose? Is there anything I can do to help?"

"I wish I could get back," she says. "That's the main thing I worry about."

I can see the sense of loss tonight in her eyes. Sometimes there's laughter in them. The times when she lets herself forget that she's a woman stuck here on someone else's estate. But tonight isn't one of those nights.

I'll probably never know what it's like. To be in her position. To be the one lost somewhere and trapped by the weather. Out of step with someone I don't even know, in a place I don't know. In my life, everything has been tailored for me. To suit me as a future earl and now as the earl.

And that's not the case for Miss Penrose. I'm well aware that that's not her reality.

There are some things that don't make sense about her. She struggled to believe I was the earl, despite my telling her twice. And sometimes she plays such strange music. I don't really know what to make of her.

Nonetheless, whoever she is, I must do everything I can to make her feel comfortable and to help her find her way back home. As the Earl of Ashendon, my duty can be nothing less.

CHAPTER SEVEN

AVA

Back in my room, I reflect on what I told Ashendon earlier. Or, more precisely, what I didn't tell him.

Part of me so badly wanted to tell him the truth about my being a witch. It's such an important part of who I am. To understand me fully, the fact that I'm a witch is essential to know.

Nonetheless, I held back the truth from Ashendon. I can't trust him yet, however many shared moments with a hint of a spark we've shared at the piano or playing cards or sharing late night cups of tea. Not everyone is accepting of witches. Neither in my own time nor in Regency England. Ashendon's era is only a few generations removed from witch burnings. Who knows what he thinks about witches?

I must keep the truth carefully guarded, for my own safety. Anything else risks catastrophic consequences.

CHAPTER EIGHT

AVA

A few days later, we're in the drawing room. It's afternoon and like so many afternoons I've spent here thus far, we're rained out with not much else to do other than find our entertainment inside.

Ashendon, for some reason best known to himself, has brought tons of his paperwork into this room over the past couple of weeks. There's correspondence of all kinds, letters and pamphlets and who knows what else. So much of it looks like rubbish to me. What can one man possibly do with that much paperwork?

Before I have a chance to ask him, his voice rings out across the room.

"Miss Penrose, isn't today so very dull?" he asks with a rhetorical note in his voice.

"Yes, I suppose it is."

He nods. Then, without any prior warning, he rolls up one of the pieces of paper nearest to him and chucks it into the small rubbish bin on the other side of the room. "Result!" he crows.

"Ashendon! Don't be so ridiculous!" I say. I quirk an eyebrow. Until now, I thought he was so proper and so serious. But this new antic shows a hitherto unseen side to him. Is this in fact a man who is capable of having fun after all?

"Whyever not?" he laughs.

I haven't really got a good reason why he shouldn't. There's not much else better to do on a rainy afternoon like this and it is his house, after all. "Because...because...it's so unlike you," I splutter.

"Perhaps there are sides to me you don't yet know, Miss Penrose." He waits a beat before continuing. "Say, how about we see who is the champion at paper throwing? A competition if you will."

I can't resist such a challenge. From an earl who is quickly losing all sense of propriety. "Very well, Ashendon. Prepare to be defeated."

"I look forward to it, Miss Penrose," he laughs.

I make my way over to the pile of papers on the desk and pick up a sheet. I roll it into a ball. It's game on.

My first piece of paper goes into the basket beautifully. I'm not the most athletic, but even I can do this.

Ashendon's features broaden into a grin. "Brava, Miss Penrose! Brava!"

I give him a nod by way of acknowledgement. For a man who said he wanted to make this a competition, he's behaving more like an admiring spectator than a worthy opponent.

Ashendon rolls up another piece of paper and throws it towards the waste paper basket. Another perfect shot.

We carry on like that, sometimes missing the basket but more often than not scoring a goal.

I throw another paper ball and it hits the nearly full basket with a hearty thud.

Ashendon lets out a laugh of amusement. "Oh well done, well done indeed!"

"Thank you," I say.

We've long since lost count of the score, if there was ever a scoring system in place to begin with. But that doesn't matter. We're having fun and that's what counts.

Yet despite the lightheartedness, I'm coming to realise something important. Ashendon isn't always the maddeningly proper earl he first appears to be on the surface. He's a person too, not some mere figurehead wearing some coronet.

He throws another wad of paper and doesn't miss. It's a perfect shot. The basket is now totally full.

"I suppose that's that," I say.

"Yes, Miss Penrose, I suppose it is," Ashendon replies.

He gets up from his chair and begins picking up the scrunched up bits of paper that didn't make it into the waste paper basket.

I stand up too. "Here, let me help you."

He turns to me and smiles. "Thank you, Miss Penrose."

With that, we turn the room back to its former state. As if the amateur basketball game never even happened.

CHAPTER NINE

AVA

It's another night in the dining room. When I first start-ed living here, we used to sit at the big grand table, but it was just ridiculous, like one of those old wooden set pieces from some costume drama.

Even Ashendon, prim and proper as he can be, had said only last week that the need for these sorts of formalities had faded away.

And I could not bring myself to disagree.

So now we sit at a smaller table, more like what I would have sat at in my own time.

The candles flicker against the polished silver of the cut-lery, throwing long golden shadows across the room.

We've had so many of these dinners together now, but tonight feels different somehow, and I can't quite place my finger on why. There's some sort of crackling sensation in the air, almost like a spark, you might say. But a spark of what, I don't know.

Unsure of what to say, I cast my gaze down at the spread on the table and then back up into Ashendon's hawklike brown eyes. "Your cook has outdone herself. I cannot recall when I've seen so many things that look so wonderful," I say.

A smile ghosts over his features. "I doubt that very much. You seem to bring a certain brightness to this house. I had forgotten what it was to dine with conversation worth hearing."

"Thank you, Ashendon."

He nods. "Miss Penrose, you are most beguiling and I would so dearly love if you could tell me something I don't know about you. Something new."

"Well, why don't you go first?"

"Very well." He nods again. "I have long harboured a secret passion. The fine arts. I would love to learn how to paint."

This has taken me by surprise. I had no idea Ashendon had an interest in being an artist. He doesn't seem the type. "Whyever haven't you learnt before?" I say.

"It wasn't exactly a priority for the education of a future earl," he says with a wry smile. "Everyone around me thought it more important that I focus on learning those requirements to be a proper gentleman. How to run an estate. Latin. Greek. Politics. Riding, shooting and so on. All very useful things. But there's nothing creative about any of it."

"Well, then. You should take it up. There's no time like the present," I say. "How could you learn? Perhaps there are tutors?"

"There are, indeed, Miss Penrose."

"Then you simply must learn! I decree it." I can feel the smile brimming on my cheeks.

"When you put it like that, how could I possibly refuse?" He takes a sip of his claret. "And you, Miss Penrose, what is something I don't know about you?" he asks with a slight, knowing curve at the corner of his mouth.

I almost want to tell him the truth. But the words 'I'm a witch' get stuck on the tip of my tongue. I still have no idea how he would react to such a revelation. As much as I'm coming to really like Ashendon, it's better I hold back. To protect him from the truth. And to keep myself safe.

But before I can form some sort of response, the butler enters the room carrying another carafe of claret.

I can't say anything while this man is here. Whatever I am about to say is for Ashendon's ears only.

The butler bustles around and refills our glasses.

Neither Ashendon nor I say a word.

Then, almost as quickly as he entered, the butler gives a bow and leaves.

The two of us are alone together. Again.

It's the big moment. I need to tell him something. Anything. But the biggest secret I'm keeping from him. The truth he cannot know. Instead, a flash of inspiration crosses my mind. I'll tell him about Mr Wemble. That's a safe bet.

"When I was nine," I begin, "I found a grey tabby cat round the back of our house. He was a stray. For reasons I can't recall, I decided to call him Mr Wemble. He'd hang around most days. Gentle but try as I might, he had no interest whatsoever in coming outside. He was definitely a man of the streets."

Ashendon quirks his lip and leans forward with interest.

I carry on sharing the tale of Mr Wemble. "But I wasn't about to let that stop me from making him the best performing cat in the whole country."

"The best performing cat?" Ashendon asks.

"Yes, performing tricks and such."

"I didn't know cats could do that," he says with a discernable note of bafflement.

"They can't. But nine year old me didn't know that. I spent weeks upon weeks trying to teach him how to fetch and beg and roll over. Like he was some kind of dog. It was all to no avail."

"What rotten luck," Ashendon says.

"I know," I laugh. "Poor Mr Wemble!"

"Poor Mr Wemble indeed."

I breathe a sigh of relief internally. Mr Wemble was a good get out of jail free card. I can only hope that Ashendon, handsome as he is, never discovers the biggest secret I'm really hiding.

Chapter Ten

Ashendon

It's just after eleven at night. And I'm making my way downstairs. I'm struggling to sleep and perhaps something from the kitchens would do me good. I'm so single-mindedly focused on getting to the kitchens that I don't realise when I bump into her in the narrow hallway that leads to the back stairs.

Well, I say bump, but really it's more of a jolting encounter. Her satin skirts brush against my legs. And it's tantalising. But I can't let my thoughts run away from me. I'm a gentleman after all.

She gasps and then laughs. "Ashendon, how nice to see you here."

"Um, yes, yes." I try to formulate a response but I'm lost for any meaningful words. Blast it. Why does one always lose one's ability to form a coherent sentence at a time like this? It's most un-Earl-like.

The satin of her skirts rustles as she shifts slightly in the hallway. "What are you doing up this late, at this hour," she asks.

"Oh, I'm heading to the kitchens. And what, pray tell, are you doing?"

"I'm trying to get back to my rooms," she says. There's a note of concealment in her voice, as though she's not telling me everything, but I'm a gentleman and she's a lady, and it would simply be too out of bounds for me to question her intentions. I'm sure she's just trying to get back to her rooms.

"Well, very good. I hope you achieve that."

"Thank you, Ashendon," she says with a little laugh.

"Good night to you then. And please do forgive me, Miss Penrose. It was not my intention to make you feel there was any risk of impropriety."

"Thank you, Ashendon," she says.

With that, she leaves me standing alone in the corridor.

I cannot imagine Miss Penrose is happy with what just happened. For her to be so close to a man at night, it's unthinkable. I really didn't mean for that to happen. It would never be my intention to compromise her. I'm an earl after all.

And yet, and yet, and yet, I can't deny that I liked it when we bumped into each other tonight. That I wish it would happen again. It would take every shred of my effort to maintain my composure, even a tiny bit of it. And I cannot jeopardise Miss Penrose's reputation. It would be too ungentlemanly of me.

She is quite simply the most confusing yet the most alluring woman I have ever had the pleasure to meet. Everything about her raises more questions than it does answers. Who is she really? Where is she from? The way she moves? The way she looks at me with some sort of question, some sort of query in her eyes that she doesn't seem to want to ask? I don't understand any of it. How did she even get here?

And all that strange talk about camels? If I knew, if I didn't know better, I would think she was...No, I won't say it. That's very rare and, well, other than my late grandmother, I've never met anyone else who was. So it seems most unlikely.

No, I think she's just a woman who's somehow gotten lost and it's my duty and responsibility to help her get back home, not to waste her time or cause fear for her with my own desires. She's not even a member of the aristocracy from what I can tell, so she's off the cards for an earl.

But, by heavens, if she was, if she was the daughter of some Viscount, or even someone from the gentry, I wouldn't hesitate to tell her how I feel.

When she brushed against me, and I know she didn't mean to, I felt a frisson. A frisson of excitement and a frisson of delight and a frisson of all the possibilities a life with someone like her can entail.

But I don't think it will ever be possible. We're from two different worlds, and it just wouldn't work. A man like me has responsibilities, including a responsibility to behave with the highest level of comportment towards women such as Miss Penrose.

I can't keep standing here like a statue, ruminating on a lady who I can never have. I need to keep busy. To focus my mind on other things. Yes, I can't let myself get distracted.

With that self-chastisement out of the way, I continue on my journey towards the kitchens.

CHAPTER ELEVEN

AVA

I sit on my bed, going through my notes on magical time travel theory for the umpteenth time.

All those lessons at Spellpath Academy and I still haven't made much progress.

Initially, I thought the Fregellei theorem held some promise. But I've tried implementing that spell five different ways and five times there's been no result whatsoever. Not even a flash of light or a shimmer of smoke. It's been so disheartening.

But I cannot give up. I will not give up.

Even if it takes me years and years, somehow I know I will find a way back to my own time. Back to the twenty-first century.

If I don't believe that, then what hope do I have?

I need hope. I need something to believe in.

So I go back to my notes and reread them for the umpteenth-and-one time. Maybe this will be the time I have a breakthrough.

CHAPTER TWELVE

ASHENDON

The wind is howling something chronic tonight. This year without a summer has been one bad day followed by one bad night in a seemingly ceaseless cycle.

I'm sitting at my desk in my study in a futile attempt to make some headway on the latest estate paperwork. My steward will be on my case again if I don't sort out these ledgers in good time.

The candle flickers and casts a warm orange glow across the ledger. I'm really trying to focus on the figures in front of me. There's the staff wages and tenant rents and the coach repairs. All very important and all things I, as an earl with duties and responsibilities, really must focus on.

But my mind is swept away by other matters. My houseguest. The mysterious Miss Penrose. I can't help but wonder what she is doing. I must make sure she is comfortable.

I can't keep looking at these papers so I raise myself from my seat and pad out into the hallway.

No sign of Miss Penrose. Perhaps she has already retired for the night. Perhaps this is all fruitless. But she's the houseguest and I want to be a good host.

Then I hear a creaking on the stairs.

I look up and it's her. Miss Penrose.

She stops and turns to cast her gaze down at me. A small smile forms on her features. "Oh! Ashendon, I didn't expect to see you here," she says.

"Nor I you," I say.

"I was about to head to bed. What are you doing up this late?"

"I've been trying to make some headway on estate paperwork. But I must admit that progress hasn't been very successful."

"Because of the wind? I hate it when it's like this."

"Exactly," I nod. "I find I can't focus at all when it's blowing a gale outside." An idea pops into my head. Perhaps it is a good idea, perhaps it is a bad one. But it wouldn't hurt to ask. Nothing ventured, nothing gained, after all. "Say, Miss Penrose, would you care to join me for a nightcap? It might help both of us find some distraction from all this blustery wind."

"Yes, why not." She makes her way down the stairs to meet me in the hallway. "Anything to take my mind off a night like this."

We make our way to my study.

I leave the door conspicuously open. Stormy weather or not, I will not do a single thing to put Miss Penrose's reputation at risk.

I head over to my drinks cabinet and pull out an old favourite. A fine port plus two glasses.

Miss Penrose leans against my solid oaken desk, careful to avoid knocking over the teeming mass of paperwork.

I walk over and hand her one of the glasses of port. Then I take a sip of my own. The rich plummy aroma fills my nostrils.

"Ashendon, may I ask you a question?" she says.

"Of course, Miss Penrose."

"Are there often nights like this, when it's hard to get to sleep?"

"Sometimes," I reply.

"Because of your estate duties?" she asks.

"When they're stressful or there's a lot going on, then sometimes yes," I say cautiously. "But sometimes for other reasons, like the weather we're having right now."

She nods. "I can see how all of those things would keep you up at night."

It's quiet in the office. But the silence in the air is companionable, not stilted.

"And you, Miss Penrose, do you often have trouble sleeping?" I ask.

She takes a sip of her glass of port before replying. "Like you, sometimes. But it's not the worries that come with running my earldom that keep me up at night." She casts me a wry smile.

"No, I would've presumed not," I respond.

"For which you would be correct." She sips on her port again. "Though, like you, when the wind gets like this it keeps me awake." She waits a beat before continuing. "And trying to figure out a way back home. However long that may take."

I take a couple of steps towards her. "I would like nothing more than to help you get home. The moment the road clears, you can be assured that I will organise the first carriage to get you to Little Battlington with all haste." I need to assure her of my gentlemanly intentions. I am the Earl of Ashendon, after all. And the Earl of Ashendon is a gentleman at all times and in all situations.

"Thank you."

The wind carries on blustering away in the background. It's an eerie howl. Like something out of *The Castle of Otranto*.

She finishes her port and walks over to meet me where I stand. "Well, I suppose I must get going. It is rather late."

I fumble to find the correct words and waste time gawking at her like a gormless fish before I finally manage to find some words and bid her goodnight.

She exits the room.

And with that, the peturbing interlude concludes and I'm left alone in my office to try once again to find something to occupy my mind on this sleepless night.

Chapter Thirteen

Ava

The muddy ground squelches beneath my feet. Gaps in the rain like this have been few and far between, so this is a rare opportunity to get outside and commune with the natural world.

I pull out my wand. I'm still fairly new to using it, but it's mine and I'm getting skilled at it. I tap it along the tree trunk, one, two, three, four times. This enchantment will bring about good weather. Something this place could definitely do with right now. Hopefully the enchantment takes effect quickly.

I step back and admire my handiwork. Though I'm still early in my training as a witch, I'm coming along well if I do say so myself.

My self-congratulations fill my ears. So I'm oblivious to anything else going on around me.

That is, until, heavy footsteps fill my ears.

"Miss Penrose, what precisely are you doing?" Ashendon's now familiar tones reverberate all around.

My stomach clenches. He wasn't meant to find out. Not like this. And perhaps not ever. But now he has.

I turn around slowly and move to hide my wand behind my back. I plaster a false smile on my face. "Oh, I'm admiring what a beautiful estate you have. Such lovely trees and wildlife. I just love nature!"

I roll my eyes internally at myself. Like that didn't sound desperate and insincere. A gushing stream of nonsense.

Ashendon isn't buying it, I can tell from the dubious look in his eyes.

"I'm glad to hear my estate pleases you, Miss Penrose," he says with an unmistakable note of scepticism.

Silence hangs heavy in the air between us.

I clutch onto my wand, hoping desperately that he doesn't notice.

But there it is. He does.

"Say, Miss Penrose, whyever do you have your hands in such a strange position?" he asks.

"Oh, it's more comfortable this way," I say.

"Funny way of being comfortable."

"Well, it's a good thing I'm the one standing like this and not you!" I retort.

He edges closer to me. "What's that you have? In your hand?"

"Nothing! I've nothing in my hand!" I do my best to keep my cool, but my voice is growing higher.

"I think you do." He's within touching distance from me now. "Miss Penrose, I think whatever you're holding in your hand is something you were using to do something to that tree behind you."

I say nothing. I'll not give him one inch of ground.

He continues speaking. "In fact, whatever you have in your hand is something you were using to cast a spell."

I freeze. Part of me knew that there was a risk of him guessing my secret. I'm not completely stupid. But I had hoped he would overlook anything he saw, and put it down to my being from a strange place. But this man, he knows more than he lets on.

I fight to keep my voice as steady and even as possible. "I don't know what you mean."

He takes a step behind me. "Yes, as I suspected. A wand."

I say nothing. I hope against hope that he isn't some kind of witch finder.

The next words that come out of my mouth take me by complete surprise.

"Yes," he says, casual as you like. "My grandmother, she had one exactly like it."

CHAPTER FOURTEEN

AVA

"Your grandmother?" My brow furrows in confusion.

"Yes, my grandmother. My mother's mother, third daughter of the Viscount of Henley."

I loosen my muscles a bit. But I'm still not sure I can trust this guy. Just because his grandma was a witch doesn't mean he's going to tolerate one on his property today. Maybe he hated his grandma, for all I know, and this is his shot at revenge.

In any case, I don't need to reply because he continues his monologue. "She was a very talented witch. Knew a lot of the ancient ways. Not that any ever passed down to me. I haven't a magical bone in my body."

I'm not surprised to hear that the magic didn't pass down to him. It's a rare enough gift as it is and often skips generations in families. My great grandmothers were both witches, but I'm the first in my family since them. It's a gift and you either have it or you don't.

"One so rarely meets witches," he continues. "I am very curious why you decided to visit me, though?"

"Well, I didn't decide," I say.

"Really? Then how are you here? Did you just appear out of thin air?" he asks, his eyes truly wide now.

The idea of my appearing out of nowhere shocks him more than my being a witch. This is interesting.

I loosen my arms a little. There's no point trying to hide the wand anymore. "Well, you see, I'm not too sure myself how I got here."

He quirks an eyebrow. "What do you mean?"

"I was out walking, to find Old Tattersham's Circle. The weather started out fine but got worse as the day wore on. It got so bad that I was considering turning back. Only there was a sudden flash of lightning. How that happened, I have no idea. And then you appeared."

"But the weather that day was fine. There wasn't any rain or lightning." He turns away from me and says nothing for several seconds.

I'm exasperated now. "I don't know why," I groan. "It just happened. It's not like I can control the weather."

"Some witches can."

"Yes they can. But they're much more experienced than me."

Silence fills the air again.

I'm not going to say anything further. He wanted to pursue this line of questioning, so let him deal with the awkwardness. It's no skin off my nose.

He turns back around to face me. He casts his eyes over me, from head to toe. "None of this makes any sense."

"Trust me, it doesn't make any sense to me either. And I would love to know why it happened and how to undo it."

"Undo it? Coming here, you mean?"

"Yes," I nod.

"But then where did you come from? If not from here. You said you were on your way to Old Tattersham's Circle. That's not two miles away!"

"Correct." I don't really want to tell him what inevitably comes next. I don't want to lay all my cards on the table. But he already knows I'm a witch and doesn't seem appalled by it, so maybe he has some old spellbooks of his grandma's kicking around that will help me get back home.

In for a penny, in for a pound. I sigh to myself, before I say, "I come from England. But not the England of your time."

"You're a time traveller?" he smacks his palm against his forehead. "That explains a lot."

I give a small smile. "It does. I thought you were an actor when I first saw you."

"An *actor*?" He's incredulous. "Whyever would you think I'm an *actor*?"

"When I come from, men only dress like you when they're acting. When they're playing the part of a gentleman from some Jane Austen drama."

His eyes light a little in recognition. "Austen. The Prince Regent loves her work. And you read some of her Sense and Sensibility to me so excellently. Well, she prefers to keep her name private but it's an open secret in society circles." He looks away at the ground. "You said, 'when I come from'. When exactly are you from, Miss Penrose?"

I tell him the year.

He shakes his head in semi-disbelief. "Yes, that explains a lot. There's something otherworldly about you."

Silence clings in the air between us.

His gaze dives deeply into mine. He's assessing. Querying. But also recognising something, like the pieces in a jigsaw are all coming together for him.

I cough in a moment of nerves. "Well, now you know the truth."

"I do, yes," he nods.

"I'm sorry I didn't tell you sooner."

"I don't blame you. Who could've possibly believed you. It sounds ludicrous. Fantastical even."

"But it's true."

"Yes, it's true," he nods.

Somewhere in the distance, skylarks are singing. But I hardly pay them any mind. My focus is on the revelation I've just made and the man who stands in front of me. Whatever am I to do? I really want to get home. So badly. An idea bursts into my head. "Your grandmother, did she leave any books behind? Books of magic? Maybe there's something in there that will help me get back to my own time."

He tilts his head a little. "She may well have, though I've not read much of them myself. You're welcome to look at them. They'll likely mean more to you than they would to me."

"I'd like that please."

"Very well. I can show you where they are now, if you'd like."

"Lead the way."

We head back into the house and a few minutes later, we're walking through the main doors.

He takes me down a couple of corridors and into a room I've never seen before. It's a small office with dark purple walls and a ceiling painted deep blue with yellow stars and a crescent moon. It looks like the night sky. The very sort of place a witch might do her bidding.

Chapter Fifteen

Ava

There are piles and piles of books to work through. The earl's grandmother had quite the collection of magical texts and tomes. The librarians at Spellpath Academy would be impressed.

Some days, the amount there is to read overwhelms me. There are books upon books upon books. From every time and from every land.

But on other days, having so much to read is sheer invigoration. There is so much magical knowledge contained within these walls and I want to drink it all in.

I spend most of my days researching and reading and researching and reading. Trying to find anything, anything that will give me a clue to finding the way out of here and getting back at last to my own time.

Usually I'm not alone. Ashendon is with me most days. Researching and reading. Researching and reading.

Neither of us have any better place to go. We're flooded in. No carriages nor any horses have been able to get through on the roads for weeks. And as for travelling on foot, that's a lost cause.

So, for want of anything else to do, the earl and I are wending our way through his grandmother's magical book collection.

We will surely find the answer to get me back home. I keep telling myself that it's only a matter of time.

CHAPTER SIXTEEN

ASHENDON

I sit at my desk in my office. It wasn't too long ago that I brought Miss Penrose in here for the first time. That day she demanded I prove to her that I'm the earl. So I showed her document after document and newspaper after newspaper until she couldn't deny the truth anymore. I am the Earl of Ashendon and I shall be until the day I die.

Every day that we've spent together during these floods has been a revelation. Before Miss Penrose arrived, my days here formed the same rhythm of estate management, riding, and hosting the occasional group of friends or family. Then, I would head down to London each year for the obligatory season. Sooner or later, after all, an earl must find a wife. But though I've been going for several years, nothing has ever stuck.

When I look at Miss Penrose, I am so taken by every inch of her. There is not a moment in the day when I don't think of her.

Some might say it's because she's different. Because she's a witch. Because she's from another time. But there's more to it than that. Whatever timeline, witch or not, she would still captivate me. The pull is too strong. The ocean is too deep.

I'm growing very fond of Ava. I can't help but think of her by that name sometimes, even though I know it is taking liberties. She is and must always remain Miss Penrose to me. Names notwithstanding, there are moments when I can't help myself but think of what it would be like for her to stay here forever with me. In 1816.

This year we're having has been intensely wild and unpredictable. Thus a witch appearing in my life has been par for the course.

Her presence, however, has made everything so much lighter. Finally, finally, my days feel like they mean something.

I wish she could stay here with me. Forever. I would like nothing more than to spend the rest of my life with her.

Yet alas! I am only being selfish.

As much as I wish for her to stay here in 1816 at Varley Hall, I know it can never be a reality.

She is not from here. She deserves to go back to her own time. To her friends and family. To where she belongs.

Keeping her here with me would only serve to please my own selfish desires. And that is something a true gentleman can never ever dare to do.

Chapter Seventeen

Ava

Although we are both trying our hardest to get through Ashendon's late grandmother's mammoth collection of magical tomes, progress is achingly slow. There are just so many books to read and so many spells to check. So far, nothing has fit the bill.

I hold up yet another likely useless tome. It's hefty and bound in rich purple leather. Silver and gold moons and stars adorn the cover. I palm through the pages, hoping hope against hope that this will finally be the book that sets us on the right path to solving the mystery of how to get me home.

Every page is packed with beautiful illustrations. Constellations of the heavens, so many plants and flowers I've never seen the like of before, and a vast menagerie of wondrous beasts.

But oh no! None of it is relevant to helping me get back to my own time. Instead, the book is the journal of Old Mother Zelenková. A witch who lived in fourteenth century Prague of whom there is no evidence of any linkage to time travel whatsoever. Respect Old Mother Zelenková as I do, she's going to be no help to me here.

I put the book down and shake my head with a sigh. Nothing we try seems to be working. Every avenue we go down proves to be only a dead end.

CHAPTER EIGHTEEN

AVA

Another day in the room of magical books. Ashendon is here with me, like most days.

He's currently sitting on the floor, rifling through a green leatherbound tome and furrowing his brow in deep concentration.

I'm supposed to be focusing on the book in front of me. Doing fastidious research like him so I can discover how to get out of this Regency world and back to my own time.

But I'm distracted today. Instead, I cast a surreptitious glance and drink in the sight of him. He looks so earnest and so focused.

Who would have thought that an earl would ever take such an interest in ancient magical spells? It's not like he can even do any magic himself!

Part of me would stay here every day with him, like this, if I could. These past weeks have been some of the best of my life. Working with someone to achieve a magical goal. Someone whose company, despite my better instincts, I am coming to really enjoy.

But then the other part of me still wants to go back to my own time. Being here, in this real life Jane Austen drama, has its perks and all. But can I really stay here forever? What about the world I came from and everything I know? All I know here is the earl.

Then again, he's quite unlike anyone I've ever met. And that's something I cannot overlook. I still don't know why I was brought here, back to 1816. I don't think it was an accident. I think that someone, somewhere, somehow, wanted to bring me here for a reason. What that reason is, I don't know for sure. But my meeting the earl could just be it. If I didn't know any better, I'd say that we fit together too well for all of this to be mere coincidence.

My heart lurches a little. I don't know what I want anymore. A month ago, if someone had said that they could send me back to my own time with a click of their fingers, I would have taken them up on their offer in a heartbeat. Now, however, I wouldn't be so quick. And a piece of me wouldn't want to take them up on their offer at all.

My head is awash with so many contradictory thoughts. I'm stuck in a swirling sea of confusion.

In front of me, the earl continues his steadfast research.

I wonder if he's as mixed up as I am? Or if he can't wait to see the back of me?

Unless I ask him, I suppose I'll probably never know. Some things simply aren't meant to be.

That's what I'm going to keep telling myself, at least.

I steel myself and turn my attention back to the book in front of me. I've got no time for feelings about a man from two hundred years before my time. No, I need to crack on and find a way home. I can't afford to keep wasting time speculating about something that will likely never come true.

Chapter Nineteen

Ava

The candle ebbs down to the last of its stub.

I've been reading for hours upon hours.

Normally, I finish for the day with the sunset. It won't do to burn myself out, after all.

But tonight is different. Tonight is the night where I've finally found a way home. At least, I think it's going to be a way for me to get home. I won't know for sure until I actually try it.

Even so, this is a major breakthrough. For weeks on end, Ashendon and I have been reading and researching and meeting with a brick wall at every turn. Except for tonight. Tonight our luck has changed.

Before me sits The Chronicle of Archimedes Sonia of Crete.

This is a book that has been thought lost for centuries. Spoken of only in rumours and many in the magical community have doubted its existence.

Within its weathered pages lies something I have expected to never actually find.

A way back to my own time.

It turns out that at least one person has been able to intentionally travel through time. And that person was the great Archimedes Sonia of Crete herself.

It won't be easy. Her method. It's going to require every ounce of magical power within me.

But I have to try. I have to believe in myself. That I'm capable of this. It's the only hope I have of getting back to my own time. Of leaving 1816.

I need to find him. I need to tell him.

This is exciting news. Yet also terrifying because I don't know how he's going to react. Part of me doesn't want to go back to my own time. Part of me hopes against hope that he begs for me to stay. That thought strikes fear into my heart. Because I might just say yes.

But I can't afford to be a coward. If nothing else, he deserves to know the truth of what I've discovered tonight. He deserves to know the facts.

I dart out of the room and hurry down the corridors. If I know Ashendon, and I know him very well indeed by now, he'll most likely be in his office.

There's not a moment to lose and I walk more quickly than I probably ever have in my life up until this point.

Mere minutes later and I'm bursting through his office door.

There he is. Seated at his desk, as per usual. Going through some tedious estate paperwork by the looks of it.

He glances up and meets my gaze. "Miss Penrose, what's happening? You do look rather excited."

"Well I have news," I say.

"What news, pray tell?"

"I believe I've finally found it. A way to travel through time." My pulse is racing with a confusing mix of joy and nerves.

His eyes widen. "Miss Penrose...Ava...that's wonderful news! How? When?"

"I read and I read and I read. Through every book in your late grandmother's collection. And then I finally found it. In the Chronicle of Archimedes Sonia of Crete. No one since her time had written anything down, so far as I've been able to find. But Archimedes Sonia did it. Over a thousand years ago."

"That's incredible!" he exclaims. "And her method? Is it easy?"

"Not at all. It involves building a time bridge," I say with a wry smile on my lips. "But I'm going to give it all I've got."

"I'm so happy for you, Miss Penrose. Genuinely I am." He stands in front of me, beaming.

"Thank you."

The air is thick and still around us. Like something important is about to break.

Ashendon seems to feel it too. His face falls a little and he casts his gaze to the floor. Then he says, almost to himself and not for my hearing, "I wasn't going to say this, but now is as good a time as any."

"Say what?" I ask.

He looks back up at me and rubs the back of his neck with one hand. Then he takes a few steps towards me, his eyes laser focused on mine all the while. "Miss Penrose. There is no other way for me to tell you this, so I must be direct. You are like no one else I have ever known. You are brilliant and you are most fantastical. That is why I have fallen in love with you."

Chapter Twenty

Ava

My heart beats faster and faster. Did he really just say that?

I have to shake my head at myself because it's true. He did. He just told me he loves me. I'm shocked. But in a good way. I never suspected this from him. He's so earnest. But my heart is torn. I don't know what I should do.

Because now I realise I love him back.

I so badly want to tell him I love him. Doing that, however, would only make things worse. Because that method I figured out for how to get back to my own time? Well, there's one snag. One almost fatal flaw.

It may not allow me to come back to 1816. Ever.

The time bridge requires so much power to even operate one way. So much power that I fear it's beyond my capabilities to ever set up the bridge again.

My stomach churns. I really wish I didn't have to say what I'm going to have to next.

But I can't lie to him. I can't mislead him. If nothing else, he deserves the truth.

The air is thick with silence.

I bite my lip before I begin to speak. "I love you too. That's why I can't believe I'm saying this."

His eyebrows shoot up. "Saying what?"

"I don't know if the time bridge will allow me to come back here. If I use it, I mean," I say in a rush.

His lips form a thin line. "Whyever should that be a problem?"

"Because it means if I try to return to my own time, we may never see each other again. I may not be able to come back to 1816."

He looks at me with an expression I can't read.

The air is tight with tension.

I can hardly breathe for the tenterhooks I'm hanging on.

His eyes are steady and his voice is firm. "I will go with you."

"Pardon?" I struggle to believe what I'm hearing.

"I said, I will go with you." His voice is firm and resolute.

"Go where?"

His lips quirk into the tiniest hint of a smile. "Why, back to your own time, of course."

"No." I shake my head. "No. No. No. No. You can't. I can't ask you to make that sacrifice."

"But I can," he says. "I can, it's my choice to make. And besides, you never even asked me to make it. This is my idea, after all."

"You can't! What if I can't get the time bridge back to 1816 working again?"

"That doesn't matter to me." His voice is resolute.

"But this is absurd! I can't ask you to give up your whole life for me!" I splutter. "What about everything you have here? What about your earldom?"

"I would rather have you in some future I don't even understand, than not have you and have all the earldoms in the kingdom."

"I can't ask you to do that."

"But you're not asking. It's my decision." His voice has some bite to it now.

"I can't expect you to make that sacrifice," I say.

"It's not your choice to make!" he retorts.

"I can't expect you to make it. You have too many responsibilities here. If I can't get that time bridge working both ways, then I'll stay here with you."

His draw drops. "You can't do that."

I keep my gaze steady on his eyes. "I can and I will."

CHAPTER TWENTY ONE

Later that day, Ashendon and I are outside heading towards the stone circle underneath the oak tree on the edge of his estate. It's the nearest location with enough magical residue for me to stand a chance of carrying out the time bridge spell successfully.

I look across to him. His face is purposeful. A man totally committed to what I'm about to try.

"Whatever happens, I have to know. I have to try to build the time bridge," I say.

He nods. "You should at least try. At least to know either way."

"Very well," I say. The sense of the gravity of this moment fills me with a wave of dread. I turn away from him and make my way to the stone circle.

I begin the spell, tapping my wand at ten different points around the ancient stones. As I do so, I recite those long-forgotten words Archimedes Sonia said all those centuries ago.

A flash of bright blue sparks erupt from the end of my wand. I've never done magic like this before, never this powerful.

Ashendon looks at me with wide eyes.

This magic is incredible. Even the stories from my teachers at Spellpath Academy, well, I don't think even most of them had magic as powerful as this.

The bridge is forming now between our two worlds. Slowly, slowly, there's blue light spinning around me. And then it goes deep into the ground.

A flash of light.

And for a brief few seconds, I can't see anything. When I am able to see again and the colours return to normal, it's like there's a portal underneath the oak tree.

And through that portal, I can see into a world that looks quite like this one. I think that's my time.

The Earl looks at me. "You've done it."

"I hope so," I reply. "I really hope so. But I need to be sure." I make my way to the portal. It looks ever so similar to this one.

The way I can test is whether my wand in this new world is going to emit the elithium spell. Because that spell was only created about ten years ago in my time. And if that works, then I know I've solved it.

Hesitantly, I walk towards the portal. It's now or never. Right before I step in, I turn to the Earl and I say, "I love you."

Right back to me, with the deepest sincerity I've ever heard anyone utter in all my life, he says, "I love you too, Ava. Whatever happens, know that I've always loved you."

I can't say anything more for fear of my eyes welling up, so I do what I must and I step straight forward into the portal. Then, I'm in a very similar scene.

I bring out my wand and I cast the elithium spell. One, two, three taps of my wand on the ground. Then three taps in the air.

Purple sparkles emit from the end of my wand. All the trees around me, all the birches and oaks, the ashes and pines, they shimmer. I can hear a faint singing, though it's not a human voice.

The elithium spell has worked. And so I know that I have made this time bridge work too.

Joy erupts on my features. I've done it. I've done it. I've done it. I can't quite believe it, but I've done it.

This means no choice has to be made. Ashendon and I, we can live wherever we want, whenever we want. We can be together always and for all time.

I run back through the portal back into 1816. "I've done it. I've done it," I exclaim.

"I heard you," he laughs. "I knew you could do it, my clever witch."

I run into his arms and he wraps me in an all-embracing hug. Then I grab his face between my hands and pull him in for a searing kiss.

He chuckles softly. "I never doubted you for a second. Never for a moment."

"I'm so glad to hear it," I say. "For a while there, I didn't think I was going to be able to get it working."

"Oh, I knew you could. I knew you could," he says. "And do you know what this means?"

"What?" I reply.

A small smile forms on his lips. Sardonic even. "Well, this means I finally get to see the time you're from. I've always wondered, ever since I met you, where and when you're from. And when I found out, I couldn't believe it. So I'm really going to have to see it with my own eyes."

"Oh, you shall," I reply.

And with that, I take him by the hand and I lead him through the portal and into the twenty-first century. You can't say that many Regency Earls have ever seen anything he's about to see.

Epilogue

Ava

A year has passed since that day, when I opened the portal bridge between our two worlds. And so much has happened since, let me tell you.

Ashendon and I, we stayed in the twenty-first century for a couple of weeks, and everything he saw was just wonders for him. I don't think he even really believed half of what I told him about modern times until he saw it with his own eyes. Well, who would really? We had these horseless carriages, cars to you and I. Something called the internet, now that was just beyond his fathoming. Plus the fact that we can fly? For a man who's come from a world that's barely invented the steam engine, that was almost unbelievable.

My magical powers mean that when he's in the twenty-first century, he doesn't have to worry about any of our modern illnesses or concerns, because as a witch, I can heal all of that anyway. So we're two people living both in our time and out of our time, but really they've become both of our homes.

We can even travel to other timelines. I've been able to build three other time bridges. One to the twenty-third century, one to the 1920s and one to the fifteenth century.

Each of these time bridges is amazing and they all work essentially the same. Ashendon doesn't like to travel too much further into the past than his time. He says, oh it's too old fashioned. But he really enjoys coming into what would be the future for him.

As for me, I find it all fascinating. I've visited witches in secret in all the different eras and by the twenty-third century the time bridge becomes pretty common in the witching world.

I've learned since coming back to the twenty-first century that 1816 was known as what is the year without a summer. That's why there was so much rain when I went there. There was just rain all year and the crops failed and it was a terrible time. Amazingly, I had no idea about it until I ended up getting sent back by that random lightning strike all those months ago.

The Earl and I, we're married now. In both 1816 and the twenty-first century. We both agreed it would be a bit hard to explain to anyone from either time why we had a marriage certificate from either 200 years in the future or 200 years in the past.

For me, 1816 will not only be the year without a summer. It's also the year a witch unintentionally traveled through time and found her everything.

ACKNOWLEDGEMENTS

First off, thank you to you the reader of this book. I hope that you enjoyed it.

To the team at Miblart, thank you for your brilliant work on the cover art.

And thank you, as always, to MD. For everything.

ABOUT THE AUTHOR

Chloe Willowfield adores all things historical romance. Ever since she was very young, she has been fascinated by how people lived in the past.

When she's not writing, you'll find her enjoying musicals, visiting local cafes or maybe even going on a hike.

You can connect with Chloe on Instagram, TikTok or Pinterest. You can also keep up-to-date by signing up for her newsletter.

Chloe can be reached via email at chloe@chloewillowfield.com. She'd love to hear from you!

SUBSCRIBE TO CHLOE'S NEWSLETTER

Scan the QR code below to subscribe to Chloe's newsletter and stay updated on the latest releases.

Visit Chloe's Website

Scan the QR code below or head to
www.chloewillowfield.com